TOEIC

練習測驗（15）

聽力錄音QR碼（1~100題）

LISTENING TEST

In the Listening test, you will be asked to demonstrate how well you understand spoken English. The entire Listening test will last approximately 45 minutes. There are four parts, and directions are given for each part. You must mark your answers on the separate answer sheet. Do not write your answers in your test book.

PART 1

Directions: For each question in this part, you will hear four statements about a picture in your test book. When you hear the statements, you must select the one statement that best describes what you see in the picture. Then find the number of the question on your answer sheet and mark your answer. The statements will not be printed in your test book and will be spoken only one time.

Statement (C), "They're sitting at a table," is the best description of the picture, so you should select answer (C) and mark it on your answer sheet.

1.

2.

GO ON TO THE NEXT PAGE.

3.

4.

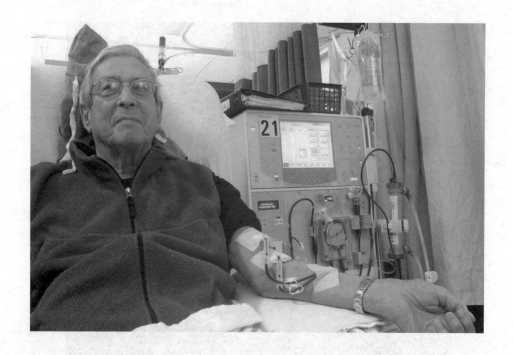

5.

© Ray Morris-Hill

6.

GO ON TO THE NEXT PAGE.

PART 2

Directions: You will hear a question or statement and three responses spoken in English. They will not be printed in your test book and will be spoken only one time. Select the best response to the question or statement and mark the letter (A), (B), or (C) on your answer sheet.

7. Mark your answer on your answer sheet.

8. Mark your answer on your answer sheet.

9. Mark your answer on your answer sheet.

10. Mark your answer on your answer sheet.

11. Mark your answer on your answer sheet.

12. Mark your answer on your answer sheet.

13. Mark your answer on your answer sheet.

14. Mark your answer on your answer sheet.

15. Mark your answer on your answer sheet.

16. Mark your answer on your answer sheet.

17. Mark your answer on your answer sheet.

18. Mark your answer on your answer sheet.

19. Mark your answer on your answer sheet.

20. Mark your answer on your answer sheet.

21. Mark your answer on your answer sheet.

22. Mark your answer on your answer sheet.

23. Mark your answer on your answer sheet.

24. Mark your answer on your answer sheet.

25. Mark your answer on your answer sheet.

26. Mark your answer on your answer sheet.

27. Mark your answer on your answer sheet.

28. Mark your answer on your answer sheet.

29. Mark your answer on your answer sheet.

30. Mark your answer on your answer sheet.

31. Mark your answer on your answer sheet.

Directions: You will hear some conversations between two people. You will be asked to answer three questions about what the speakers say in each conversation. Select the best response to each question and mark the letter (A), (B), (C), or (D) on your answer sheet. The conversation will not be printed in your test book and will be spoken only one time.

2. What are the speakers waiting for?
   (A) To enter a contest.
   (B) To hear the results of a contest.
   (C) To meet the winner of the contest.
   (D) To read the entries in the contest.

3. What is implied about the woman?
   (A) She entered the contest.
   (B) She works in publishing.
   (C) She was the favorite to win the contest.
   (D) She has a changeable temperament.

4. How does the woman feel?
   (A) Confident.
   (B) Angry.
   (C) Bored.
   (D) Doubtful.

5. Where are the speakers?
   (A) In a public park.
   (B) In a government building.
   (C) In a sporting arena.
   (D) In a whirlwind romance.

6. What does the woman want?
   (A) A document.
   (B) To file a complaint.
   (C) A haircut.
   (D) To appear in court.

37. What will the woman most likely do next?
   (A) Call the judge.
   (B) Stay in Room 112.
   (C) Go to Room 212.
   (D) Pay the fee.

38. What position does Maria hold?
   (A) Janitor.
   (B) Gardener.
   (C) Housemaid.
   (D) Mechanic.

39. What problem does the man have?
   (A) His bushes need to be trimmed.
   (B) He can't pay Maria until Thursday.
   (C) He isn't happy with Maria's service.
   (D) He ran out of personal checks.

40. What will happen on Saturday?
   (A) Maria will plant more flowers.
   (B) The man will write a personal check.
   (C) The man will go to the bank.
   (D) Maria will get paid.

41. Why are the speakers traveling to Boston?
   (A) To settle an argument.
   (B) To save money.
   (C) To attend a conference.
   (D) To sell products.

42. When does Louise's flight leave for Boston?
   (A) Yesterday.
   (B) Today.
   (C) Tuesday evening.
   (D) Wednesday morning.

43. What does the woman suggest?
   (A) Call the airline soon.
   (B) Wait until Wednesday.
   (C) Use a different airline.
   (D) Skip the conference.

GO ON TO THE NEXT PAGE.

```
╔══════════════════════════════════════╗
║           Nellie's Diner             ║
║           Lunch Menu                 ║
║                                      ║
║  Salads                              ║
║                                      ║
║  Chef's Salad   $8      Taco Salad $8║
║                                      ║
║  Soups                               ║
║                                      ║
║  Tomato                     cup $2   ║
║  Soup of the Day           bowl $5   ║
║                                      ║
║  Sandwiches — served with fries or   ║
║                 potato chips         ║
║                                      ║
║  Roast beef, Chicken or Ham    $7    ║
║  Vegetable                     $6    ║
║                                      ║
║  Burgers — served with fries or      ║
║              potato chips            ║
║                                      ║
║  Hamburger                     $7    ║
║  Cheeseburger                  $7.50 ║
║  Bacon Cheeseburger            $8    ║
╚══════════════════════════════════════╝
```

44. What do the women agree to do?
- (A) Go to another restaurant.
- (B) Order soup and salad.
- (C) Pay for the man's lunch.
- (D) Share a large salad.

45. What does the man mean when he says "hit the spot"?
- (A) It is a great spot to eat.
- (B) A burger would satisfy him.
- (C) He would like to get his food quickly.
- (D) The woman is correct about the salad.

46. Look at the graphic. How much will the man pay for his food?
- (A) $7.50.
- (B) $8.00.
- (C) $11.50.
- (D) $15.50.

47. Who are the speakers?
- (A) Doctor and patient.
- (B) Student and teacher.
- (C) Supervisor and employee.
- (D) Brother and sister.

48. What did the woman do with the updated files?
- (A) She gave them to the secretary.
- (B) She put them on the man's desk.
- (C) She left them at home.
- (D) Nothing.

49. What did the woman do with the purchasing receipts?
- (A) She lost them.
- (B) She paid them.
- (C) She sent them to the accounting department.
- (D) She left them on the man's desk.

50. What does Kenny want?
- (A) A job on the second shift.
- (B) To punch out at midnight.
- (C) To place a holiday order.
- (D) The employee time cards.

51. What does Rachel say?
- (A) She is working the second shift.
- (B) She doesn't have all the time cards yet.
- (C) She told Mr. Edwin about the holiday.
- (D) She doesn't understand the problem.

52. What will Rachel do tomorrow?
- (A) Bring the time cards to Mr. Edwin.
- (B) Call Kenny to come and get the time cards.
- (C) Return the time cards to the employees.
- (D) Place her holiday orders.

CINEPARK THEATER			
The Great Escape	6:15	8:20	10:45
Bond Returns Again	6:20	8:45	11:00
Love's All That	6:00	8:00	10:00
Harry Houdini	7:30	10:30	
The Final Battle	7:00	9:00	11:00

53. What kind of movies does the woman like?
(A) Thrillers.
(B) Romantic comedies.
(C) Action movies.
(D) Horror movies.

54. Look at the graphic. What time will the speakers see a movie?
(A) 9:00.
(B) 6:00.
(C) 8:45.
(D) 6:20.

55. Why does the woman suggest a compromise?
(A) She and the man have different tastes in movies.
(B) She would like to pay for the movie tickets.
(C) She promised that she would see the Bond movie.
(D) The war movie is too long.

56. Who are the speakers?
(A) Strangers.
(B) Co-workers.
(C) Employer and employee.
(D) Friends.

57. What happened to the man?
(A) He lost his wallet.
(B) He lost his job.
(C) He lost his house keys.
(D) He lost his dog.

58. What does the man imply?
(A) His former employer is making a lot of money.
(B) Some of his co-workers lost their jobs, too.
(C) He should have paid the taxi driver.
(D) His manager is finding new jobs.

59. What is the relationship between the speakers?
(A) Salesperson and customer.
(B) Teacher and student.
(C) Husband and wife.
(D) Boss and employee.

60. What is the man's problem?
(A) The order wasn't placed yesterday.
(B) Too many people have attended the seminar.
(C) He doesn't have enough money to pay the bill.
(D) He is late for an appointment.

61. What does the woman suggest?
(A) Order more soda.
(B) Choose a different sandwich.
(C) Move the lunch period.
(D) Cancel the seminar.

GO ON TO THE NEXT PAGE.

Online Registration

Name*	Ann Temple
Student number*	43981286
E-mail address	
Phone number*	
Address	Room 207
	Shaw Dormitory
Course number*	A402
Section number*	12

* indicates required field

SUBMIT

62. What is the woman trying to do?
   (A) Submit a paper.
   (B) Register for a room in the dormitory.
   (C) Find out what time her class starts.
   (D) Enroll in a course.

63. What does Gary suggest?
   (A) The class will not fit her schedule.
   (B) The class might be full.
   (C) The woman is not good at using computers.
   (D) The online registration system has many problems.

64. Look at the graphic. Why was the woman unsuccessful?
   (A) She did not click SUBMIT.
   (B) She did not write her home address.
   (C) She did not fill in her e-mail address.
   (D) She did not fill in her phone number.

65. What is the man's problem?
   (A) He might be getting sick.
   (B) He needs a ride home.
   (C) He wants to be free.
   (D) He lost his job.

65. What will the man do tomorrow morning?
   (A) Go to work.
   (B) Go to class.
   (C) Take a vacation.
   (D) See a doctor.

67. What does the woman say?
   (A) She approves of the man's decision.
   (B) She does not approve of the man's decision.
   (C) She wants to go along with the man.
   (D) She does not believe the man has a problem.

68. What does Katrina imply to Otis?
   (A) He is a lazy employee.
   (B) He should have been fired a long time ago.
   (C) He will find another job quickly.
   (D) He may have an opportunity to get his job back.

69. Who are the speakers?
   (A) Doctor and patient.
   (B) Student and teacher.
   (C) Supervisor and employee.
   (D) Brother and sister.

70. What does Otis suspect?
   (A) He's about to be promoted.
   (B) He's about to be fired.
   (C) He's about to get a raise.
   (D) He's about to take a vacation.

PART 4

Directions: You will hear some talks given by a single speaker. You will be asked to answer three questions about what the speaker says in each talk. Select the best response to each question and mark the letter (A), (B), (C), or (D) on your answer sheet. The talks will not be printed in your test book and will be spoken only one time.

1. What is the speaker mainly discussing?
   (A) Entertainment.
   (B) Geography.
   (C) Economics.
   (D) Weather.

2. What happened in Okinawa?
   (A) It was struck by a tornado.
   (B) At least 50 people were injured.
   (C) Only three people were injured.
   (D) Five people were killed.

3. What did NOT happen in Japan?
   (A) Many homes lost electricity.
   (B) There were strong winds.
   (C) People were injured.
   (D) The government declared an emergency.

4. Who is the speaker?
   (A) An expert on statistics.
   (B) An expert on communication.
   (C) An expert on corporate management.
   (D) An expert on body language.

5. What will the speaker talk about?
   (A) Listening skills.
   (B) Speaking skills.
   (C) Study habits.
   (D) Management styles.

6. When can the audience ask questions?
   (A) At the end of the speech.
   (B) Before the speech begins.
   (C) 30 minutes later.
   (D) Any time.

77. Where is this announcement being made?
   (A) At a sports stadium.
   (B) In an airport.
   (C) In a restaurant.
   (D) At a public auction.

78. What is the speaker offering?
   (A) A prize package.
   (B) An internship.
   (C) An autographed basketball.
   (D) A chance to play for the Bulls.

79. Which of the following is NOT mentioned by the speaker?
   (A) Big Al's Restaurant.
   (B) Derrick Rose.
   (C) Pink Panda Car Wash.
   (D) The name of the winner.

80. When was this report made?
   (A) In the early morning.
   (B) In the afternoon.
   (C) At noon.
   (D) In the evening.

81. What will happen tomorrow?
   (A) It will rain.
   (B) Lane closures on I-45.
   (C) A slight breeze off the lake.
   (D) A parade on Fuller Road.

82. Where would this report be heard?
   (A) On the radio.
   (B) In a newspaper.
   (C) On the Internet.
   (D) On the voice mail system.

GO ON TO THE NEXT PAGE.

County Bus Routes

Avery	8:00	9:15	4:30	5:15
Casper	7:00	7:15	7:30	8:00
Freeport	8:00	9:30	11:00	12:30
Milltown	8:00	10:00	12:00	2:00
Polk City	6:30	7:00	12:00	3:00
Trallee	8:15	9:15	10:15	11:15

83. What does David suggest?
  (A) Leaving early for Honest Traders.
  (B) Going to Honest Traders after one o'clock.
  (C) Leaving for Polk City later in the day.
  (D) Going to a different place than planned.

84. What is the disadvantage of going to Freeport?
  (A) It is farther away.
  (B) It is difficult to return from.
  (C) It is too crowded.
  (D) The store has limited hours.

85. Look at the graphic. Which bus would David like to take?
  (A) The 10:15 to Trallee.
  (B) The 7:00 to Polk City.
  (C) The 12:00 to Milltown.
  (D) The 9:30 to Freeport.

86. What is prohibited by law?
  (A) Using laptops in the cabin.
  (B) Tampering with smoke detectors.
  (C) Listening to music on the flight.
  (D) Carry-on luggage.

87. Where does this announcement take place?
  (A) On an airplane.
  (B) At a business meeting.
  (C) On television.
  (D) In a bus station.

88. What should listeners do if they have a question?
  (A) Call the airline.
  (B) Ask a flight attendant.
  (C) Go to the lavatory.
  (D) Complain to the manager.

89. What will the speaker most likely talk about next?
  (A) Sports.
  (B) The weather.
  (C) Biology.
  (D) Economics.

90. Where did the speaker obtain his master's degree?
  (A) Bio-Tech.
  (B) University of Illinois.
  (C) Northwestern University.
  (D) Stanford University.

91. Where was the speaker born?
  (A) Boston.
  (B) Chicago.
  (C) Russia.
  (D) Illinois.

2. Who is the speaker?
   - (A) A preacher.
   - (B) An animal therapist.
   - (C) An author of comic books.
   - (D) A advertising professional.

3. Why does the speaker tell the story of the donkey?
   - (A) To draw a comparison.
   - (B) To explain a procedure.
   - (C) To clarify a statement.
   - (D) To insult an audience member.

4. What does the speaker say about average consumers?
   - (A) They look like donkeys.
   - (B) They are overwhelmed by choice.
   - (C) They prefer smaller bales of hay.
   - (D) They have a passion for creativity.

5. What is the speaker mainly discussing?
   - (A) His reason for starting a business.
   - (B) His political views.
   - (C) His experience with computers.
   - (D) His opinion of the computer industry.

6. What does the speaker say about consumers?
   - (A) They don't care about customer service.
   - (B) They prefer reliable companies.
   - (C) They give him a competitive edge.
   - (D) They always think they can do a better job.

97. What does the speaker imply about his company?
   - (A) They provide a high level of customer service.
   - (B) They are most concerned with competitive pricing.
   - (C) They are struggling.
   - (D) They are wildly profitable.

98. What is the purpose of this announcement?
   - (A) To announce an event.
   - (B) To sell a product.
   - (C) To start an argument.
   - (D) To introduce a speaker.

99. What is implied about the 4th of July?
   - (A) It's a minor religious holiday.
   - (B) It's an important American holiday.
   - (C) It's an excuse to set fires.
   - (D) It's a reason to become an American.

100. What should customers do if they want a free shot?
   - (A) Bring at least three friends.
   - (B) By an appetizer.
   - (C) Wear something red, white, and blue.
   - (D) Pay the admission fee in advance.

This is the end of the Listening test. Turn to Part 5 in your test book.

GO ON TO THE NEXT PAGE.

READING TEST

In the Reading test, you will read a variety of texts and answer several different types of reading comprehension questions. The entire Reading test will last 75 minutes. There are three parts, and directions are given for each part. You are encouraged to answer as many questions as possible within the time allowed.

You must mark your answers on the separate answer sheet. Do not write your answers in your test book.

PART 5

Directions: A word or phrase is missing in each of the sentences below. Four answer choices are given below each sentence. Select the best answer to complete the sentence. Then mark the letter (A), (B), (C), or (D) on your answer sheet.

101. The last bus to Taichung ------- at 11:30.
(A) departs
(B) depart
(C) departing
(D) to depart

102. Remember kids: don't answer the door for anyone ------- you know who they are.
(A) except
(B) unless
(C) because
(D) instead

103. The event is ------- the public, with proceeds from ticket sales benefiting a children's art education fund.
(A) open on
(B) opened at
(C) opening of
(D) open to

104. His stories are so colorful that they defy -------.
(A) landing
(B) applause
(C) description
(D) change

105. A newly ------- Spanish-language channel called Latino TV is wholly dedicated to traveling.
(A) launching
(B) launce
(C) launched
(D) launch

106. The museum has an amazing ------- of Vincent van Gogh's artwork.
(A) handicap
(B) collection
(C) directive
(D) tasting

107. Marty can play guitar ------- piano.
(A) because of
(B) by and by
(C) if not for
(D) as well as

108. Taking the flu seriously also ------- taking annual vaccinations seriously.
(A) involves
(B) requests
(C) kneels
(D) confirms

14

09. When it comes to life insurance, it ------- to quit smoking.
(A) spits
(B) runs
(C) pays
(D) longs

10. Life is a ------- struggle; there is no easy ------- to success.
(A) constant ; path
(B) pleasant ; line
(C) mindless ; button
(D) career ; step

11. The noise coming from next door ------- their romantic dinner.
(A) closed
(B) invited
(C) upgraded
(D) disrupted

12. Mr. Peterson has ------- learned to send e-mails and chat with friends on social media.
(A) yet
(B) already
(C) no
(D) ever

13. Jason smiled and waved as he walked -------.
(A) instead
(B) from
(C) found
(D) past

14. Seth doesn't seem to be ------- failing another exam.
(A) combined with
(B) complained to
(C) concerned about
(D) contracted by

115. The weather forecast ------- more rain and wind.
(A) demands
(B) respects
(C) calls for
(D) remembers

116. You must study hard for the college entrance exam. There is a lot -------.
(A) of cake
(B) to take
(C) at stake
(D) to break

117. After the war, many radicals and traitors were -------.
(A) completed
(B) executed
(C) made
(D) performed

118. All those daydreams were only -------; they disappeared one by one.
(A) contemptuous
(B) contemplate
(C) temporary
(D) contemporary

119. One of the ------- aspects of the new headquarters is its closeness to the downtown area.
(A) pleasing
(B) pleased
(C) pleases
(D) please

120. Greg keeps a detailed ------- of all his personal financial transactions.
(A) credit
(B) bank
(C) account
(D) receipt

GO ON TO THE NEXT PAGE.

121. With pleasant weather, breathtaking views and a ------- tourist industry, California's 1,350 miles of sunny shoreline are a significant source of commerce and state pride.
(A) well-furnished
(B) well-developed
(C) well-beloved
(D) well-adjusted

122. Raised in Panama, 41-year-old ------- Hannah Hooper first moved to New York to study fashion merchandise at the Parsons School of Art and Design.
(A) architect
(B) architecture
(C) art
(D) arcade

123. Although Mr. Darby is a good counselor, a few changes in his approach ------- both him and his clients.
(A) should disturb
(B) might terrify
(C) would benefit
(D) have enrich

124. You will report ------- to the manager and you will be responsible for supervising the work of engineers and designers.
(A) direct
(B) directly
(C) direction
(D) directed

125. Shouting profanities is not a(n) ------- response to this situation.
(A) live
(B) casual
(C) suggestive
(D) appropriate

126. You realize that looking good on the outside isn't necessarily ------- being healthy, don't you?
(A) at length with
(B) the same as
(C) to part with
(D) as told to

127. Unfortunately, ------- who suffer during an economic recession are typically the poorest members of society.
(A) this
(B) that
(C) them
(D) those

128. Though this week's sales were relatively -------, the stock price of Linda's Toys continued to fall.
(A) height
(B) high
(C) highly
(D) heighten

129. Throughout the course of the experimen we can quickly ------- the relationship between temperature and volume by changing the value for one or the other.
(A) revoke
(B) dispose
(C) establish
(D) found

130. Anderson spoke with actress Mayim Bialik, who ------- a Ph.D. in neuroscience.
(A) holded
(B) hold
(C) holding
(D) holds

PART 6

Directions: Read the texts that follow. A word, phrase, or sentence is missing in parts of each text. Four answer choices are given below each of the texts. Select the best answer to complete the text. Then mark the letter (A), (B), (C), or (D) on your answer sheet.

Questions 131-134 refer to the following advertisement.

Is your fur baby looking a little shaggy these days? -------?
131.

Perfect Pet has the solution! We ------- full grooming services
132.

for any breed of dog, including Heinz 57. Our groomers have

experience with ------- cuts from classic poodle to English
133.

sheepdog. We also offer bathing, teeth cleaning, and nail

trimming. So bring in your pup today and take home a Perfect

Pet. Services are available ------- or on a walk-in basis.
134.

Perfect Pet

126 Main Street

(across from Bailey Supermarket)

Phone: 589-2000

Hours: 9am-7pm

---

131. (A) Does your coat have unsightly stains on it
    (B) This is the new style this year
    (C) Does your dog absolutely hate baths
    (D) Of course, babies should not wear fur

132. (A) make
    (B) offer
    (C) distribute
    (D) afford

133. (A) a couple of
    (B) the number of
    (C) both of
    (D) a variety of

134. (A) as soon as possible
    (B) by appointment
    (C) with nomination
    (D) on the fly

GO ON TO THE NEXT PAGE.

To:	All administrative staff
From:	Frank Wheeler
Subject:	New printing facilities
Date:	May 15, 2020

Callum Corporation has installed new printers and copiers in Suites 814, 1002, and 1206. These ------- will be operational
135.
as of Monday, May 18. The IT department has installed the printers on the PCs of all administrative assistants. You will be able to print remotely from your workstations. You should use the printing suite on the floor that is closest to your workstation. You will ------- that the printers have been named 8A, 8B, 10A,
136.
and so on, to ------- their location. As always, printers and copiers
137.
may be used for company business only. -------.
138.

Frank Wheeler
Office Manager

135. (A) abilities
    (B) administrators
    (C) facilities
    (D) institutions

136. (A) find
    (B) determine
    (C) notify
    (D) require

137. (A) notice
    (B) discover
    (C) involve
    (D) reflect

138. (A) If your company has any business, please call the number below.
    (B) In that case, you should ask your assistant for a new printer.
    (C) If you experience any technical difficulties, please contact the IT department.
    (D) All printers will be on sale until the end of them month.

Dear friends and patrons,

Your support for the St. Simons Bakery has been outstanding.
-------, we have enjoyed a booming business. That means we have
139.
------- our current location. In order to continue to serve you in a
140.
clean and comfortable environment, we are moving to a new—and
much larger!—location. Our new store is just two blocks away on
Mill Street, between First and Second Avenue. In order to ------- the
141.
move, we will be closed for three days, from August 1 – August 3.
We will have a Grand Opening at our new location on August 4
with free coffee and samples of our delicious baked goods. -------.
142.

Our store hours will remain the same: 7:00 am – 8:00 pm.

139. (A) At no time
(B) In due course
(C) Thanks to you
(D) Begging your pardon

140. (A) outdone
(B) outlived
(C) outworked
(D) outgrown

141. (A) motivate
(B) facilitate
(C) dedicate
(D) collaborate

142. (A) We look forward to seeing you there
(B) You can move in at any time
(C) We expect you to come on time
(D) We can all get along with the new manager

GO ON TO THE NEXT PAGE.

Adam Williamson

1246 Maple Drive

Springfield, MA 50119

Dear Mr. Williamson,

After examining our records, we noticed that you are ------- three books
143.

that are considerably overdue for return. As you know, the ------- of our
144.

books may be checked out for two weeks. You may keep the books longer if

you wish, but you must come into the library to extend the lending time. In

addition, books that are not returned by their due date ------- fines of 25 cents
145.

per day per book. Your books are currently three weeks overdue. -------. If
146.

you have any questions, feel free to contact me by phone.

Sincerely,

Rosemary Evans

Head Librarian

Springfield Lending Library

143. (A) having
  (B) in need of
  (C) in possession of
  (D) overtime with

144. (A) most
  (B) majority
  (C) percentage
  (D) number

145. (A) infer
  (B) imply
  (C) invest
  (D) incur

146. (A) I will visit the client in the afternoon
  (B) Please bring your bag to the office
  (C) I forgot to mention that you look good
      today
  (D) Please visit the library at your earliest
      convenience to resolve this issue

Directions: In this part you will read a selection of texts, such as magazine and newspaper articles, e-mails, and instant messages. Each text or set of texts is followed by several questions. Select the best answer for each question and mark the letter (A), (B), (C), or (D) on your answer sheet.

Questions 147-148 refer to the following advertisement.

A Christmas Concert
At the National Concert Hall

Address: No. 21 Zhōngshān S. Road,

Zhōngzhèng District, Taipei

Time: December 24 at 7:30 pm

Price at door: 800 TWD

Prepaid Price: 500 TWD

Phone: (02) 2578-6731

Renowned Canadian conductor Howard Dyck leads

the Taipei Symphony Orchestra in a family-friendly

Christmas concert that will fill your heart with

Christmas cheer! Don't miss this holiday treat!

147. What is the purpose of this ad?
(A) To sell a product.
(B) To promote a concert.
(C) To announce a new holiday.
(D) To recruit potential employees.

148. Where will the event be held?
(A) The National Concert Hall.
(B) 7:30 p.m.
(C) 800 TWD.
(D) December 24.

GO ON TO THE NEXT PAGE.

Summer is the best time to return to school!
You need better business skills and we can help.

Each summer Rockland College of Business Administration offers special courses for experienced managers who want to sharpen their existing business skills or learn new ones. You will study with your peers in a week-long intensive session that simulates the world of international commerce. You will learn new theories and study market trends from around the world. Students in previous sessions have found this knowledge to be immediately applicable to their current work situations.

Only one student per company is accepted into this special program. All applications require three letters of recommendation and employment verification.

For more information, call the **Summer Training Center**
College of Business Administration
Rockland College
(212)372-3477

149. Who would most likely be interested in this advertisement?
(A) Office clerks.
(B) Professional managers.
(C) College professors.
(D) Undergraduate students.

150. What is required for admission?
(A) Your college transcripts.
(B) Your college diploma.
(C) Three letters of recommendation.
(D) Above average test scores.

menu

Lounge Bar

garlic bread	2.50
fat chips	5.00
potato wedges	6.00
rib fillet steak sandwich w chips	11.00
cajun chicken strips w salad & chips	11.00
bangers & mash w vegetables	11.00
garlic prawns w rice	12.00
rissoles w sweet potato mash & vegetables	11.00
roasted pumpkin, spinach & ricotta ravioli w parmesan cream sauce	12.00
caesar salad	10.00
chicken caesar salad	12.50
roast of the day* lunch	3.50
dinner	10.00

THURSDAY NIGHT SPECIAL

t-bone, salad & chips*	7.99

prices subject to change

*only available with drink purchase

51. What is the least expensive item on the menu?
(A) Garlic bread.
(B) Fat chips.
(C) Roast of the day at lunch.
(D) Potato wedges.

152. What is the most expensive item on the menu?
(A) Garlic prawns with rice.
(B) Chicken Caesar Salad.
(C) Roast of the day at dinner.
(D) Ravioli with parmesan cream sauce.

GO ON TO THE NEXT PAGE.

Dear Libby,

I am 24 and graduated from college with a bachelor's degree in criminal justice. I am currently living with my parents. They are a bit controlling and hate resistance from me. I grew up doing everything they told me with no personal opinions of my own, until I met my fiancé a year ago. He has helped me gain the strength to speak up and let my thoughts be known.

We're trying to save enough money to live together. Mom has made it clear that she doesn't like that idea because we're not married yet. She and Dad are also unhappy that I no longer want to work in the field my degree is in. (I worked for a sheriff's office for a couple of months and was treated horribly, and then I was fired.)

I have told my parents repeatedly that this is my life, but it seems to do no good. Do you have any suggestions on what I should say to them about these issues?

– GROWN-UP GIRL IN GEORGIA

153. What is Grown-up Girl's main problem?
(A) Control issues with her daughter.
(B) Control issues with her employer.
(C) Control issues with her parents.
(D) Control issues with her boyfriend.

154. What does Grown-up Girl want to do?
(A) Get married.
(B) Choose a new major.
(C) Move in with her boyfriend.
(D) Have a child.

 We hate to break it to you, but big companies aren't just going to let a chilly employee crank the heat up whenever he or she pleases. But if they simply locked the thermostat or put the controls out of reach, the employees would constantly complain. The solution: A thermostat that doesn't actually do anything but placate the chilly masses.

In many offices the controls on the wall don't do anything. Some bosses and landlords feel like they can't trust people not to fiddle with the temperature all day and thus cost them money, so they install dummy thermostats which give people the illusion of control. They work really well, as most people fool themselves into believing they feel the change.

When pressed, most technicians tasked with installing the devices admit that they're merely window dressing. A 2010 report by *The Wall Street Journal* quoted one HVAC technician who estimated that 90% of office thermostats were completely fake (though other technicians gave lower estimates). We haven't seen any study confirming that people feel warmer after fiddling with these props. But let's be honest: If they didn't work, offices wouldn't bother installing them.

155. What is the purpose of the article?
(A) To expose a little known fact.
(B) To draw support for a cause.
(C) To explain a complex procedure.
(D) To demand an apology.

156. What supports his claim?
(A) An employee survey.
(B) Scientific research.
(C) Public opinion.
(D) An article in *The Wall Street Journal*.

157. What does the author claim?
(A) All bosses and landlords are cheap.
(B) All employees are not to be trusted.
(C) Most office thermostats are merely props.
(D) Most HVAC technicians are dishonest.

GO ON TO THE NEXT PAGE.

As the name implies, fast-food is supposed to be, well, *fast*. But have you ever wondered what the fastest fast-food restaurant is?

According to Quick Service Restaurant (QSR) Magazine's annual Drive-Thru Performance Study of six national fast-food chains, Wendy's takes the crown with an average 129.75 seconds per transaction. Burger King came in sixth, barely hanging onto its crown with 201.33 seconds.

By averaging the times during 318 visits to Wendy's, QSR Magazine found that Wendy's was 20 seconds faster than second-place Taco Bell. The magazine and Insula Research conducted the survey by visiting each restaurant between 203 to 362 times. However, speed may not be everything.

The fast-food industry doesn't exactly have an equivalent to the computer chip industry's Moore's law, which predicted in the 1970s that processing power would double every two years. Complex menus have contributed to a plateau in drive-thru speed for the last seven or eight years, the magazine states. A statement from Burger King noted that it "prides itself on providing excellent products and great service to all of our guests."

QSR's other ratings included order accuracy, favorable exterior, condition of landscaping, speaker clarity and customer service. Here is its ranking of restaurants by average service times:

1. Wendy's – 129.75 seconds
2. Taco Bell – 149.69 seconds
3. Bojangles' – 171.61 seconds
4. Krystal – 175.94 seconds
5. McDonald's – 190.06 seconds
6. Burger King – 201.33 seconds

158. What was the main focus of the QSR study?
(A) Average service times.
(B) Affordability.
(C) Order accuracy.
(D) Exterior conditions.

159. What did Moore's Law predict?
(A) Declining customer service.
(B) The growth of computer processing power.
(C) Exploding profit margins.
(D) Improved speaker clarity.

160. What has caused drive-thru service times to plateau?
(A) Complex menus.
(B) Customer complaints.
(C) Longer lines in the drive-thru.
(D) Poorly trained employees.

Memorandum

TO: Kelly Anderson, Marketing Executive
FROM: Jonathon Fitzgerald, Market Research Assistant
DATE: June 14
SUBJECT: Fall Clothes Line Promotion

Market research and analysis show that the proposed advertising media for the new fall line need to be reprioritized and changed. Findings from focus groups and surveys have made it apparent that we need to update our advertising efforts to align them with the styles and trends of young adults today. No longer are young adults interested in television shows. Also, it is has become increasingly important to use the Internet as a tool to communicate with our target audience to show our dominance in the clothing industry.

XYZ Company needs to focus advertising on Internet sites that appeal to young people. According to surveys, 72% of our target market uses the Internet for five hours or more per week. The following list shows in order of popularity the most frequented sites:

- Google
- Facebook
- Myspace
- eBay
- iTunes

Shifting our efforts from our other media sources such as radio and magazine to these popular Internet sites will more effectively promote our product sales. Young adults are spending more and more time on the Internet downloading music, communicating and researching for homework and less and less time reading paper magazines and listening to the radio. As the trend for cultural icons goes digital, so must our marketing plans.

61. What is the main purpose of this memo?
  (A) To propose a change to a plan.
  (B) To attract young readers.
  (C) To announce a new product.
  (D) To discipline a group of employees.

62. Who wrote the memo?
  (A) A marketing executive.
  (B) An advertising sales person.
  (C) A market research assistant.
  (D) A group of concerned adults.

163. According to the memo, which of the following is the most popular website?
  (A) Google.
  (B) Facebook.
  (C) eBay.
  (D) iTunes.

GO ON TO THE NEXT PAGE.

WHO Health Guidelines for Your Pre-Schooler

Nothing is more important than your child's health. [1] This week, the World Health Organization released new guidelines for the youngest of our children, those under the age of five. In general, the guidelines say that children should both move more and sleep more. [2] Specifically, kids between the ages of one and four should be physically active for at least three hours a day. Infants should also be active several times a day. As every parent knows, getting enough sleep is key to growing up healthy both physically and mentally. Four-year-olds generally need 10 to 12 hours of sleep a day, those under the age of one need 12 to 15 hours. What's not included in the WHO guidelines? [3] Screen time. In fact, according to the WHO, children aged two to four should spend no more than one hour a day looking at an electronic screen. Kids younger than that shouldn't be watching screens at all. How does one balance that with the demands of young kids for video entertainment? [4] Well, that's what parenting is all about.

164. What is the article about?
(A) How to limit screen time for pre-schoolers.
(B) Tips for raising healthy children.
(C) WHO guidelines on sleep deprivation.
(D) When children should begin using computers.

165. What does the author suggest?
(A) Parents are responsible for following these guidelines.
(B) The WHO guidelines are unrealistic.
(C) It is impossible to make children follow the guidelines.
(D) The WHO should include more practical advice in its guidelines.

166. What does the WHO recommend for a typical two-year-old?
(A) Frequent exercise, but no access to electronic screens.
(B) More than an hour a day of television but more than 12 hours of sleep.
(C) No television at all and more exercise and sleep.
(D) Three hours of physical activity and at least 10 hours of sleep each day.

167. In which of the positions marked [1], [2], [3], and [4] does the following sentence best belong?
"It is worthwhile, therefore, to listen to the experts."
(A) [1]
(B) [2]
(C) [3]
(D) [4]

Silver was the most popular exterior car color in America for nearly a decade. But while it remains beloved by automotive designers for best showing off a car's styling, it was finally overthrown this year by white. According to Sandy McGill, BMW Designworks' lead designer in color, materials, and finish, this is Steve Jobs' doing. "Prior to Apple, white was associated with things like refrigerators or the tiles in your bathroom. Apple made white valuable."

Valuable, yet boring. Fortunately, our expert interviews and analysis reveal that more enticing colors are emerging.

Light blue's ascension is connected to environmental wellbeing: clear skies, clean water. Crisp oranges are migrating from the world of high-end outdoor equipment. New paint technology may finally allow fashion's passion for fluorescents to flow from the runways onto the highways. And, as always, the smart money's on gold: as its price and profile have skyrocketed, so has its demand as a coating.

68. Where would this article most likely be found?
(A) A website about cars.
(B) A fashion magazine.
(C) An academic journal.
(D) A marketing report.

69. According to the article, who is responsible for the popularity of the color white?
(A) Automotive designers.
(B) Luxury car dealers.
(C) Insurance companies.
(D) Steve Jobs.

170. What does the author think about the color white?
(A) It is exciting.
(B) It is boring.
(C) It is dangerous.
(D) It is unpopular.

171. Which of the following is not mentioned the article as an enticing color?
(A) Scarlet red.
(B) Fluorescent.
(C) Light blue.
(D) Gold.

GO ON TO THE NEXT PAGE.

On Monday, July 27th, the residents of the Big Apple witnessed something quite out of this world: three men gracefully flying around the skies of Lower Manhattan. As it turns out, they were not ballet dancers with super human powers, but cleverly camouflaged radio controlled airplanes.

The gimmick was the genius idea of Thinkmodo, a New York-based marketing company that specializes in concocting viral sensations to promote events. This recent one was created to publicize the release of *Chronicle*, a movie about three high-school students who discover they have super powers that include the ability to fly.

The three people-planes each completed six, five-minute flights across the Hudson River. Though "kite-like" in appearance and weight (just 4 lbs. each), the planes were actually sophisticated flying instruments that required some expert maneuvering to ensure a smooth flight. The company therefore summoned the experts from the Academy of Model Aeronautics, who put each radio-controlled aircraft through some rigorous testing prior to the big event.

As you can imagine, the stunt was a huge success, despite the fact that one of the "flying" men seemed to lose his super power mid-flight and had to be fished out of New York City's Harbor Point. Fortunately, for those of us who missed it, there is a great video that captures the salient moments.

This is not the first time Thinkmodo has come up with such a stunt. To promote the recent thriller *Limitless*, they released a video depicting a man using an invention to hack the large video screens that line New York City's Times Square.

72. What is Thinkmodo?

(A) A radio-controlled aircraft.

(B) An aeronautics academy.

(C) A marketing company.

(D) A movie producer.

73. What did people in Lower Manhattan witness on July 27?

(A) Three ballet dancers in a street brawl.

(B) Three men flying though the sky.

(C) Three men flying a plane.

(D) A marketing stunt involving radio-controlled airplanes.

174. What was Thinkmodo trying to promote?

(A) Environmental awareness.

(B) Its brand name.

(C) A movie entitled *Chronicle*.

(D) The Academy of Model Aeronautics.

175. What is true about Thinkmodo?

(A) They had to be fished out of Harbor Point.

(B) They have done this type of thing before.

(C) They are very picky when choosing clients.

(D) They are a nonprofit corporation.

GO ON TO THE NEXT PAGE.

Article 1

The number of uninsured U.S. residents has grown to over 45 million (although this number includes illegal immigrants). Since health care premiums continue to grow at several times the rate of inflation, many businesses are simply choosing not to offer a health plan, or if they do, to pass on more of the cost to employees. Employees facing higher costs themselves are often choosing to go without health coverage. Health care has become increasingly unaffordable for businesses and individuals. Businesses and individuals that choose to keep their health plans must pay a much higher amount. Remember, businesses only have a certain amount of money they can spend on labor. If they must spend more on health insurance premiums, they will have less money to spend on raises, new hires, investment, and so on. Individuals who must pay more for premiums have less money to spend on rent, food, and consumer goods; in other words, less money is pumped back into the economy. Thus, health care prevents the country from making a robust economic recovery. A simpler government-controlled system that reduces costs would go a long way in helping that recovery.

Article 2

There isn't a single government agency or division that runs efficiently; do we really want the government handling something as complex as health care? Quick, try to think of one government office that runs efficiently. Fannie Mae and Freddie Mac? The Department of Transportation? The Social Security Administration? The Department of Education? There isn't a single government office that squeezes efficiency out of every dollar the way the private sector can. We've all heard stories of government waste such as million-dollar cow flatulence studies or the Pentagon's 14 *billion* dollar Bradley design project that resulted in a transport vehicle which when struck by a mortar produced a gas that killed every man inside. How about the U.S. income tax system? When originally implemented, it collected 1 percent from the highest-income citizens. Look at it today. A few years back the government published a "Tax Simplification Guide," and the guide itself was over 1,000 pages long! This is what happens when politicians mess with something that should be simple. Think about the Department of Motor Vehicles. This isn't rocket science—they have to keep track of licenses and basic database information for state residents. However, the costs to support the department are enormous, and when was the last time you went to the DMV and didn't have to stand in line? If it can't handle things this simple, how can we expect the government to handle all the complex nuances of the medical system? If any private business failed year after year to achieve its objectives and satisfy its customers, it would go out of business or be passed up by competitors.

GO ON TO THE NEXT PAGE.

176. What is the main difference between the two articles?

(A) Subject matter.
(B) Use of language.
(C) Opinion.
(D) There is no difference.

177. What do both articles agree on?

(A) The government is highly efficient.
(B) Health care is expensive.
(C) Taxes are too high.
(D) They don't agree on anything.

178. What does the first article say?

(A) The government should control the health care system.
(B) Taxes should be raised.
(C) More research is needed.
(D) Most people don't have insurance.

179. What does the second article say?

(A) People choose to go without insurance.
(B) The government should not be trusted to control the health care system.
(C) The private sector will destroy health care.
(D) Health insurance is not practical for small businesses.

180. Which of the following is NOT discussed in either article?

(A) Health care.
(B) Insurance.
(C) Business.
(D) Politics.

Date: Mon, 15 June 2020

To: "**Craig Stevenson**" <blaze@facebook.com>,

   "**David Ward**" <geezer@msn.com>,

   "**Bob Dobbins**" <bobber@aol.com>

From: "**Brent Heinrich**" <bheinrich@gmail.com>

Subject: Re: Weekend in Hualien

Craig, et al.

I once went on a hiking excursion with heavy weather brewing offshore, and we chose to proceed despite the possibility of heavy rain. We ended up having to call in a rescue team.

The east coast highway is prone to flooding and rockslides, and this is not a joke. So I'd appreciate it if you'd can the mockery, Craig. If the typhoon has passed by this weekend and the coast is clear (literally and figuratively), then fine, let's have a beach party. Otherwise, let's not be chuckleheaded dimwits.

The forecast was for the typhoon to land today, but it has not reached Taiwan yet. That means it's moving slower than expected. The likelihood of a serious storm being on top of the island this weekend is high. If so, I'm not driving down the east coast.

If you choose to do so, I pity those who travel with you. We all know your old clunker has no air-con, and you have to drive with the windows open.

GO ON TO THE NEXT PAGE.

Date: Mon, 15 June 2020

To: "**Brent Heinrich**" <bheinrich@gmail.com>,

"**Craig Stevenson**" <blaze@facebook.com>,

"**Bob Dobbins**" <bobber@aol.com>

From: "**David Ward**" <geezer@msn.com>

Subject: Re: Weekend in Hualien

Brent,

First of all, it's Monday. A lot can happen between now and Friday. Given the general reliability of weather forecasting, there's no reason to panic and cancel the trip unless it is clearly a dangerous storm. If you really want to take the discussion in that direction, I find it funny that you've chosen to ignore the reports which indicate the typhoon isn't coming anywhere near the east coast. (<u>Click here</u> for that report. You're welcome.)

Second, nobody said anything about hiking in remote mountain areas. We're not camping in Taroko Gorge, for God's sake. Remember? We've booked rooms at a beach resort. Golf, swimming, poker, eating and drinking are on the agenda.

Finally, even if you had not been sarcastic and bitter toward Craig, your "chuckleheaded dimwits" comment would be offensive if I took anything you say seriously. Your choice of words pretty much sums up your character. Therefore, I personally feel that this trip would be infinitely more enjoyable if you weren't a part of it. So please, honor your promise to stay home.

81. Who wrote the first e-mail?
    (A) Brent Heinrich.
    (B) Craig Stevenson.
    (C) David Ward.
    (D) Bob Dobbins.

82. Who wrote the second e-mail?
    (A) Brent Heinrich.
    (B) Craig Stevenson.
    (C) David Ward.
    (D) Bob Dobbins.

83. What does the author of the first e-mail say?
    (A) Craig is a terrible driver.
    (B) The typhoon will probably miss the east coast.
    (C) It is too dangerous to take the trip.
    (D) They need to call in a rescue team.

184. What does the author of the second e-mail say?
    (A) The highways along the east coast are closed.
    (B) Weather forecasts are almost always accurate.
    (C) Craig isn't going to drive.
    (D) Brent should stay home.

185. What is the purpose of the trip?
    (A) To escape the typhoon.
    (B) To engage in recreational activities.
    (C) To go hiking in the mountains.
    (D) To report on the storm.

GO ON TO THE NEXT PAGE.

Ridgewood to Get New City Park
Feb. 15, 2020

City council members approved funds for a new municipal park at last night's meeting. Funds for the park's construction will come from a penny sales tax on all purchases made in the city, except for food and medicine. The park is planned for the Oak Leaf district. Unsurprisingly, there was some objection to the new tax from residents of other districts. However, Mayor Baker has assured citizens that future improvement projects are in the works for other city districts.

Dear Mayor Baker,

I am a resident of Oak Leaf, where the new park was recently opened. While I applaud your efforts to improve the environment of our city, I would like to make you aware of some unintended consequences of this new park.

We all appreciate having a green area to enjoy, but the park has drawn visitors from all over the city. Of course, every citizen has the right to enjoy the park, but parking has become a real problem in the area. Cars are often illegally parked around the neighborhood and they cause a lot of inconvenience for the residents. In addition to that, many of these visitors bring noise and leave their trash behind. When the park first opened, it was a beautiful place to relax. Now it is often littered with paper and other trash.

I hope that you can address these problems so that we can all enjoy Ridgewood's parks.

Sincerely,
Joe Smith

Oak Leaf Park
Rules and Regulations

1. **Park hours: 7AM – 10PM**
2. **No parking on streets bordering the park. Please use the lot at Green St. and Long Brook Road.**
3. **No littering. Please use the provided trash bins.**
4. **All dogs must be on a leash.**
5. **No loud music at any time.**
6. **No fires.**

Thank you for your cooperation.

86. Why did Joe Smith write the letter?
    (A) To express his appreciation for the park.
    (B) To suggest some rules for the park.
    (C) To complain about some behaviors in the park.
    (D) To protest the increase in the sales tax.

87. Why do people from other areas of the city visit Oak Leaf Park?
    (A) They paid for its construction.
    (B) There are no other parks in the city.
    (C) It is an attractive park.
    (D) In order to dump their trash.

88. Which of the following is closest in meaning to the phrase "unintended consequences"?
    (A) Unexpected outcomes.
    (B) Accidental damage.
    (C) Unfair penalties.
    (D) Impolite behavior.

189. What does Joe Smith mean when he says "address these problems"?
    (A) The mayor should allow only people living in Oak Leaf to use the park.
    (B) The mayor should make a speech about the problem.
    (C) The mayor should reply to Joe's letter.
    (D) The mayor should do something about the problems.

190. How many of the regulations are related to the problems that Joe Smith mentioned?
    (A) Two.
    (B) Three.
    (C) Five.
    (D) Six.

GO ON TO THE NEXT PAGE.

IAAC 2020 Online Registration	
* indicates required field.	
Name*	
Organization	
Address	
E-mail*	
Phone Number	
Have you attended IAAC before?	☐ Yes ☐ No
I will attend*	☐ October 15 ☐ October 16 ☐ October 17
Registration Fee*	☐ Single-day registration $75.00 ☐ Two-day registration $125.00 ☐ Three-day registration $160.00

To:	registration@IAAC.org
From:	jmcdaniels@ucanberra.edu
Subject:	Registration questions
Date:	July 1, 2020

I am writing this e-mail to inquire about your refund policy. I plan to attend two days of the conference, October 16-October 17. However, with the conference so far off, it is difficult for me to be 100 percent sure of my travel itinerary. I am currently scheduled to arrive in Madrid on October 15, but I may be delayed by one day. Therefore, I may miss the second day. In that case, would I be entitled to a partial refund of my two-day registration? I would appreciate a speedy response as I know the conference tickets are in high demand.

Sincerely,

James McDaniels, Ph.D.
University of Canberra

To:	jmcdaniels@ucanberra.edu
From:	lprescott@IAAC.org
Subject:	Registration questions
Date:	July 2, 2020

Dear Dr. McDaniels,

Thank you for your interest in the conference and for your question. You are correct in thinking that the tickets are in high demand. Therefore, I would like to explain your options so that you can make your decision as soon as possible.

As stated on our website, all conference tickets are non-refundable and non-transferrable. Therefore, if you purchase a two-day registration and are able to attend only one day, you will not be eligible for a refund of the unused portion. You could purchase only a single-day registration for October 17. That would give you the flexibility to purchase another single-day ticket for October 16 if you are able to attend. However, there is a good chance that there may be no tickets available on that day. My advice to you, if finances allow, is to go ahead and purchase the two-day registration in order to ensure that you can attend all of the activities you wish.

If I can be of any further assistance, please do not hesitate to contact me.

Sincerely,

Lee Prescott

GO ON TO THE NEXT PAGE.

191. What will happen in Madrid on October 15, 2020?
(A) James McDaniels will arrive in Madrid.
(B) Registration for the IAAC will be completed.
(C) An international conference will begin.
(D) Mr. McDaniels will confirm the dates that he will attend the IAAC.

192. What problem does James McDaniels have?
(A) He cannot attend the conference.
(B) He cannot afford to pay the three-day registration fee.
(C) He was denied a discount on the registration fee.
(D) He does not know exactly when he will arrive in Madrid.

193. If Dr. McDaniels registers for two days, but attends only one, how much will he pay?
(A) $75.
(B) $150.
(C) $125.
(D) $50.

194. Which of the following must be filled in on the form in order to register for the conference?
(A) The name of the organization one represents.
(B) A phone number where one can be contacted.
(C) The dates that one wishes to attend.
(D) One's previous experience with IAAC conferences.

195. Why does Lee Prescott advise Dr. McDaniels to register for two days?
(A) Day two of the conference is the most important day.
(B) All registration fees are non-refundable.
(C) There is a limit to the number of tickets available.
(D) Day two of the conference is already sold out.

Dear Parents,

Spring is here, and it is time to start planning our annual Crafts Fair. As you know, the proceeds of the fair will go toward funding interesting field trips and outings for children in grades 4 through 6. The fair will be Saturday, April 25, so there is still lots of time to create some projects for sale. We're looking for any hand-made item, from pots to banana bread. If you're not the crafty type, don't worry. There are lots of other ways you can help make the fair a success. We'll be holding our first organizational meeting next Thursday at 4:00 in room 303. Come out and support our school!

Melanie Carter
PTA president

My son / daughter _____ in _____'s
                        (child's name)   (teacher's name)

class has my permission to attend the school field trip on May 10. I understand that I should pick up my child from school no later than 4pm on May 10.

☐ I am available to attend this field trip as a chaperone.

☐ I am not available to attend this field trip as a chaperone.

Parent's signature: _____ Date: _____

GO ON TO THE NEXT PAGE.

Dear Ms. Albertson,

Thank you for showing me and my classmates your museum yesterday. I had a really good time, and I learned a lot. I liked the shark exhibit the most. They were really big and cool. I'm going to study more about sharks. I want to be an ocean scientist when I grow up. Maybe I can help the sharks and the other sea creatures.

Sincerely,

Billy Taylor

196. When was Melanie's letter most likely written?
(A) April 25.
(B) March 15.
(C) May 10.
(D) May 1.

197. Where did the students most likely go on May 10?
(A) The zoo.
(B) An art museum.
(C) A water park.
(D) A natural science museum.

198. Why did Billy Taylor write his letter?
(A) To ask for a scholarship.
(B) To express appreciation.
(C) To arrange a visit.
(D) To submit his homework.

199. What does Melanie Carter mean by "not the crafty type"?
(A) Honest.
(B) Not very intelligent.
(C) Not interested in art.
(D) Not good at making things.

200. What does the word "chaperone" as used in the form most likely mean?
(A) Supervisor.
(B) Driver.
(C) Teacher.
(D) Parent.

Stop! This is the end of the test. If you finish before time is called, you may go back to Parts 5, 6, and 7 and check your work.

NO TEST MATERIAL ON THIS PAGE

GO ON TO THE NEXT PAGE.

New TOEIC Listening Script

PART 1

1. (   ) (A) The cord is twisted around the kettle.
   (B) The induction cooker is plugged into the outlet.
   (C) The man wants an outlet for his energy.
   (D) A plug has been pulled out of the outlet.

2. (   ) (A) The house's upper windows are open.
   (B) A banner is hanging from the ceiling.
   (C) Chimneys rise above the roofs.
   (D) Men are climbing the ladder.

3. (   ) (A) The windows are wide open.
   (B) The flower box shades the window.
   (C) The trees are in front of the windows.
   (D) The plants are growing in the window box.

4. (   ) (A) Some notes are stuck to the monitor.
   (B) The factory's output is monitored for defective items.
   (C) The nurse is monitoring the patient's condition carefully.
   (D) The patient is connected to the monitor.

5. (   ) (A) This is a cheesecake.
   (B) This is a chess tournament.
   (C) He likes chasing girls.
   (D) He likes chewing gum.

6. (   ) (A) The professor is giving a lecture.
   (B) The dancers are performing on a stage.
   (C) The pedestrians are crossing the street.
   (D) The salesman is signing a contract.

PART 2

7. (   ) It's dark in here. Would you mind if I turned on a light?
  (A) Suit yourself.
  (B) Make up your mind.
  (C) Bite the bullet.

8. (   ) Which one is your girlfriend?
  (A) Up.
  (B) The one on the right.
  (C) We're single.

9. (   ) Why are the maintenance guys here?
  (A) To test the smoke alarms.
  (B) Once a week or so.
  (C) The short one is the brains of the operation.

10. (   ) How's the weather there?
  (A) Gorgeous.
  (B) Superstitious.
  (C) Awkward.

11. (   ) Does Robert have a bad temper?
  (A) Yes, the temperature went up to 30°C.
  (B) No, I seldom lost my temper.
  (C) Yes, he is so grumpy.

12. (   ) How long do you plan to stay?
  (A) About two more days.
  (B) I arrived with my friends.
  (C) We'll have to change our plans.

13. (   ) Are you familiar with an agent named Mr. Mulder?
  (A) No, I've never heard of him.
  (B) Yes, I need a travel agent.
  (C) Yes, you and I are very similar.

GO ON TO THE NEXT PAGE.

14. (　　) Will you have time to visit the factory?
    (A) Denmark.
    (B) We make them.
    (C) No, maybe next time.

15. (　　) Do you come here often?
    (A) Tomorrow.
    (B) He's the owner.
    (C) No, this is my first time.

16. (　　) Have you ever tried stinky tofu?
    (A) Let's have something to eat.
    (B) No. What does it taste like?
    (C) Yes. I have tried them all.

17. (　　) Do you have any sales experience?
    (A) The class starts tomorrow.
    (B) Loveable.
    (C) No, I don't.

18. (　　) Where are you from?
    (A) I'm from central Pennsylvania.
    (B) I know where you're coming from.
    (C) I haven't seen him lately.

19. (　　) How long were you locked out of the house?
    (A) The door was locked.
    (B) I forgot my key.
    (C) About an hour.

20. (　　) Didn't you go to high school with Marcy?
    (A) I graduated in 2020.
    (B) No, we went to high school together.
    (C) Yes, we were classmates.

21. (　　) How many orders did we receive?
    (A) Good night. Drive safely.
    (B) Over three hundred.
    (C) Advice is better to give than to receive.

2. (   ) What did you think of Irene?
    (A) Think again, my friend.
    (B) Her name is Irene.
    (C) I thought she was very nice.

3. (   ) You'll never guess who I saw at the shopping mall!
    (A) What?
    (B) Who?
    (C) How much?

4. (   ) Why are you breathing so hard?
    (A) I ran all the way home.
    (B) I just woke up.
    (C) I need something to drink.

5. (   ) Did you read the contract before you signed it?
    (A) What deep wound ever healed without a scar?
    (B) No, that's what babysitters are for.
    (C) Yes, I read it over twice.

6. (   ) You were born in Atlanta, weren't you?
    (A) It's about an hour from Macon.
    (B) I was there yesterday.
    (C) Yes, I was.

7. (   ) Were there many guests at your party?
    (A) About fifty.
    (B) They seemed to be happy.
    (C) Not more than twenty dollars.

8. (   ) What happened to your shirt?
    (A) Stripes aren't my style.
    (B) It fits very well.
    (C) I spilled paint on it.

9. (   ) How did the client react to your presentation?
    (A) I voted for Eisenhower twice.
    (B) They seemed to be very impressed.
    (C) I looked for their reactions.

GO ON TO THE NEXT PAGE.

30. (　　) Did you see Norman at the party?
　　　　(A) It was a party.
　　　　(B) Yes, he was there.
　　　　(C) Only Norman.

31. (　　) Who is in charge of ordering the office supplies?
　　　　(A) Check with the secretary.
　　　　(B) There is a stapler on my desk.
　　　　(C) Friday night.

PART 3

Questions 32 through 34 *refer to the following conversation.*

M : Have they announced the winners of the writing contest?

W : Not yet. I heard it won't be until after lunch.

M : You must be very anxious.

W : Well, there were so many contestants and talented competitors. I'm not sure how I rate against them, so I haven't got my hopes up, I can tell you that.

32. (　　) What are the speakers waiting for?
　　　　(A) To enter a contest.
　　　　(B) To hear the results of a contest.
　　　　(C) To meet the winner of the contest.
　　　　(D) To read the entries in the contest.

33. (　　) What is implied about the woman?
　　　　(A) She entered the contest.
　　　　(B) She works in publishing.
　　　　(C) She was the favorite to win the contest.
　　　　(D) She has a changeable temperament.

34. (　　) How does the woman feel?
　　　　(A) Confident.
　　　　(B) Angry.
　　　　(C) Bored.
　　　　(D) Doubtful.

M : Is this the Department of Records?

W : This is the Archives and Records Center. What exactly are you looking for?

M : I need a certified copy of my name change decree.

W : OK, well, that would be on the second floor. Room 212. They handle certifications. Do you have your case number?

M : No, the judge said I wouldn't need it. The information sheet he gave me says to come here, to Room 112, with a valid driver's license, pay the fee, and that's it.

35. (   ) Where are the speakers?
      (A) In a public park.
      (B) In a government building.
      (C) In a sporting arena.
      (D) In a whirlwind romance.

36. (   ) What does the woman want?
      (A) A document.
      (B) To file a complaint.
      (C) A haircut.
      (D) To appear in court.

37. (   ) What will the woman most likely do next?
      (A) Call the judge.
      (B) Stay in Room 112.
      (C) Go to Room 212.
      (D) Pay the fee.

M : Thanks for all your hard work, Maria. The yard looks fantastic, and it's nice to have the bushes trimmed. However, I was wondering if you could do me a small favor.

W : I'll try, sir.

M : Could you please hold this check until Thursday? I don't get paid until then, and I don't want it to bounce.

W : That's going to be a problem, sir. You see, I don't usually accept personal checks for my work. Strictly cash. But I'll tell you what. How about if I come back on Saturday and you can pay me then?

GO ON TO THE NEXT PAGE.

M : OK, that's a fair deal. Thanks for understanding. Come by Saturday morning and I'll have the cash ready for you.

38. (   ) What position does Maria hold?
    (A) Janitor.
    (B) Gardener.
    (C) Housemaid.
    (D) Mechanic.

39. (   ) What problem does the man have?
    (A) His bushes need to be trimmed.
    (B) He can't pay Maria until Thursday.
    (C) He isn't happy with Maria's service.
    (D) He ran out of personal checks.

40. (   ) What will happen on Saturday?
    (A) Maria will plant more flowers.
    (B) The man will write a personal check.
    (C) The man will go to the bank.
    (D) Maria will get paid.

Questions 41through 43 *refer to the following conversation.*

W : Hey, Brian. Have you booked your flight to the conference in Boston yet?

M : Not yet, Louise. I haven't decided if I should fly on Tuesday evening or Wednesday morning.

W : I'm on the Tuesday evening flight. I want to get settled in the hotel and rest a little bit before the conference begins on Wednesday.

M : That's a good idea. Maybe I'll do the same.

W : I suggest you call the airline sooner rather than later. When I booked my ticket this morning the agent told me the flight was almost sold out.

41. (   ) Why are the speakers traveling to Boston?
    (A) To settle an argument.
    (B) To save money.
    (C) To attend a conference.
    (D) To sell products.

42. (　　) When does Louise's flight leave for Boston?
　　　　(A) Yesterday.
　　　　(B) Today.
　　　　(C) Tuesday evening.
　　　　(D) Wednesday morning.

43. (　　) What does the woman suggest?
　　　　(A) Call the airline soon.
　　　　(B) Wait until Wednesday.
　　　　(C) Use a different airline.
　　　　(D) Skip the conference.

uestions 44 through 46 refer to the following conversation with three speakers.

/1: You're going to love this place. Everything is delicious and the portions are very generous.

| : Mm. A cheeseburger would sure hit the spot. How about you, Ann?

/2: I'd like a bowl of soup and a salad.

/1: The chef's salad is delicious but it's very big. I'm not sure I could eat anything else with that.

| : Well, I just want fries with my burger. Hey, why don't you two split a big salad and each order something else to go with it?

/2: Great idea!

/1: Yeah, I'll do that, and I'll order a ham sandwich for myself.

44. (　　) What do the women agree to do?
　　　　(A) Go to another restaurant.
　　　　(B) Order soup and salad.
　　　　(C) Pay for the man's lunch.
　　　　(D) Share a large salad.

45. (　　) What does the man mean when he says "hit the spot"?
　　　　(A) It is a great spot to eat.
　　　　(B) A burger would satisfy him.
　　　　(C) He would like to get his food quickly.
　　　　(D) The woman is correct about the salad.

GO ON TO THE NEXT PAGE.

46. (   ) Look at the graphic. How much will the man pay for his food?
 (A) $7.50.
 (B) $8.00.
 (C) $11.50.
 (D) $15.50.

Nellie's Diner
Lunch Menu

Salads

Chef's Salad $8   Taco Salad $8

Soups

Tomato   cup $2
Soup of the Day   bowl $5

Sandwiches — served with fries or potato chips

Roast beef, Chicken or Ham $7
Vegetable $6

Burgers — served with fries or potato chips

Hamburger $7
Cheeseburger $7.50
Bacon Cheeseburger $8

Questions 47 through 49 _refer to the following conversation._

M : Have you finished updating the files I gave you?

W : Yes, they're on your desk.

M : How about the missing purchasing receipts? Were you able to locate them?

W : I sure was. I sent them up to accounting as per your instructions.

M : Well done. Why don't you take the rest of the day off?

47. (   ) Who are the speakers?
 (A) Doctor and patient.
 (B) Student and teacher.
 (C) Supervisor and employee.
 (D) Brother and sister.

48. (　　) What did the woman do with the updated files?
    (A) She gave them to the secretary.
    (B) She put them on the man's desk.
    (C) She left them at home.
    (D) Nothing.

49. (　　) What did the woman do with the purchasing receipts?
    (A) She lost them.
    (B) She paid them.
    (C) She sent them to the accounting department.
    (D) She left them on the man's desk.

Questions 50 through 52 *refer to the following conversation.*

M : Hi, Rachel. Mr. Edwin sent me to pick up the employee time cards. Have you received all of them?

W : Hi, Kenny. Almost. I'm still waiting on a few from the second shift. Those guys don't punch out until midnight. Mr. Edwin knows that.

M : Actually, I think he forgot. We've got our hands full upstairs, you know, processing all the holiday orders.

W : I understand, Kenny. Tell Mr. Edwin I'll run the time cards up to his office first thing in the morning.

50. (　　) What does Kenny want?
    (A) A job on the second shift.
    (B) To punch out at midnight.
    (C) To place a holiday order.
    (D) The employee time cards.

51. (　　) What does Rachel say?
    (A) She is working the second shift.
    (B) She doesn't have all the time cards yet.
    (C) She told Mr. Edwin about the holiday.
    (D) She doesn't understand the problem.

52. (　　) What will Rachel do tomorrow?
    (A) Bring the time cards to Mr. Edwin.
    (B) Call Kenny to come and get the time cards.
    (C) Return the time cards to the employees.
    (D) Place her holiday orders.

GO ON TO THE NEXT PAGE.

Questions 53 through 55 *refer to the following conversation with three speakers.*

M1: So which movie do we want to see?

W : How about Love's All That? I hear it's a great comedy.

M2: Ugh. Please, not another romantic comedy. I'd rather see The Final Battle.

W : You know I hate war movies. How about the new Bond movie as a compromise?

M1: I'll go along with that, but we have to go to the early show. I need to be home by nine.

W : Fine with me.

M2: Me, too!

53. (   ) What kind of movies does the woman like?
    (A) Thrillers.
    (B) Romantic comedies.
    (C) Action movies.
    (D) Horror movies.

54. (   ) Look at the graphic. What time will the speakers see a movie?
    (A) 9:00.
    (B) 6:00.
    (C) 8:45.
    (D) 6:20.

CINEPARK THEATER			
The Great Escape	6:15	8:20	10:45
Bond Returns Again	6:20	8:45	11:00
Love's All That	6:00	8:00	10:00
Harry Houdini	7:30	10:30	
The Final Battle	7:00	9:00	11:00

55. (   ) Why does the woman suggest a compromise?
    (A) She and the man have different tastes in movies.
    (B) She would like to pay for the movie tickets.
    (C) She promised that she would see the Bond movie.
    (D) The war movie is too long.

V : Hi, Tom. How's it going?

 : Terrible, Sue. I just lost my job!

V : Oh, that is terrible. What happened?

 : Apparently, the company is downsizing. A bunch of us got laid off last week.

56. (   ) Who are the speakers?
      (A) Strangers.
      (B) Co-workers.
      (C) Employer and employee.
      (D) Friends.

57. (   ) What happened to the man?
      (A) He lost his wallet.
      (B) He lost his job.
      (C) He lost his house keys.
      (D) He lost his dog.

58. (   ) What does the man imply?
      (A) His former employer is making a lot of money.
      (B) Some of his co-workers lost their jobs, too.
      (C) He should have paid the taxi driver.
      (D) His manager is finding new jobs.

V : All right, Mr. Swift. Let me repeat your order. You want two cases of Coke—one diet and one regular; 50 one-serving bags of potato chips—original flavor; and 50 ham and cheese sandwiches. Is that correct?

 : Yes, it is. And can I expect that to arrive before noon? It's for attendees of our seminar.

V : That's going to be somewhat of a stretch, Mr. Swift. Even though I've got my whole crew on the sandwiches, we're looking at 12:30—at the earliest. Perhaps you could move the lunch period back to 1:00, just to be safe?

 : Well, I know this is a last-minute order. Someone forgot to take care of it yesterday—that's not your fault. I suppose there's nothing to do but move the lunch period back to 1:00.

V : Tell you what—just to ease a bit of your pain, how about if I throw in an extra 50 chocolate chip cookies, on the house?

GO ON TO THE NEXT PAGE.

59. (　　) What is the relationship between the speakers?
    (A) Salesperson and customer.
    (B) Teacher and student.
    (C) Husband and wife.
    (D) Boss and employee.

60. (　　) What is the man's problem?
    (A) The order wasn't placed yesterday.
    (B) Too many people have attended the seminar.
    (C) He doesn't have enough money to pay the bill.
    (D) He is late for an appointment.

61. (　　) What does the woman suggest?
    (A) Order more soda.
    (B) Choose a different sandwich.
    (C) Move the lunch period.
    (D) Cancel the seminar.

Questions 62 through 64 refer to the following conversation with three speakers.

W1: Help! I can't get this online registration to work!
M : Maybe the course is already full.

W2: Yeah, I had that problem with one of my classes.
W1: Oh, no! I really need this class! And this is the only section that fits my schedule.

M : Wait, I see the problem. You missed one of the boxes.
W2: Gary's right. See there? You need to fill that in. Then click submit.

62. (　　) What is the woman trying to do?
    (A) Submit a paper.
    (B) Register for a room in the dormitory.
    (C) Find out what time her class starts.
    (D) Enroll in a course.

63. (　　) What does Gary suggest?
    (A) The class will not fit her schedule.
    (B) The class might be full.
    (C) The woman is not good at using computers.
    (D) The online registration system has many problems.

64. (   ) Look at the graphic. Why was the woman unsuccessful?
    (A) She did not click SUBMIT.
    (B) She did not write her home address.
    (C) She did not fill in her e-mail address.
    (D) She did not fill in her phone number.

Online Registration	
Name*	Ann Temple
Student number*	43981286
E-mail address	
Phone number*	
Address	Room 207 Shaw Dormitory
Course number*	A402
Section number*	12
* indicates required field	
	SUBMIT

Questions 65 through 67 refer to the following conversation.

M : My throat hurts. I think I may be coming down with something.

W : Have you been to see a doctor?

M : Not yet. I have an appointment for tomorrow morning.

W : Good. It's always better to nip these things in the bud.

65. (   ) What is the man's problem?
    (A) He might be getting sick.
    (B) He needs a ride home.
    (C) He wants to be free.
    (D) He lost his job.

66. (   ) What will the man do tomorrow morning?
    (A) Go to work.
    (B) Go to class.
    (C) Take a vacation.
    (D) See a doctor.

GO ON TO THE NEXT PAGE.

67. (   ) What does the woman say?
    (A) She approves of the man's decision.
    (B) She does not approve of the man's decision.
    (C) She wants to go along with the man.
    (D) She does not believe the man has a problem.

Questions 68 through 70 _refer to the following conversation._

M : Hi, Katrina. You wanted to see me?

W : Yes, Otis. Please, have a seat.

M : Is everything OK? I feel kind of strange. You've never asked me to sit in your office before
     Am I getting fired?

W : Well, you see, Otis. You're doing a fantastic job and I think you're a great asset to this
     company. Fired is not a word I like to use. No... how shall I put this? We are offering you
     a temporary unpaid vacation, that is, until business picks up and we can bring you back
     onboard.

68. (   ) What does Katrina imply to Otis?
    (A) He is a lazy employee.
    (B) He should have been fired a long time ago.
    (C) He will find another job quickly.
    (D) He may have an opportunity to get his job back.

69. (   ) Who are the speakers?
    (A) Doctor and patient.
    (B) Student and teacher.
    (C) Supervisor and employee.
    (D) Brother and sister.

70. (   ) What does Otis suspect?
    (A) He's about to be promoted.
    (B) He's about to be fired.
    (C) He's about to get a raise.
    (D) He's about to take a vacation.

uestions 71 through 73 *refer to the following news report.*

At least 50 people were injured and 271,400 households were left without power after Typhoon Jelawat struck Okinawa island of Japan, disaster officials there said Saturday. As the storm roared toward other Japanese islands, three people were injured in the southernmost part of Kyushu, the Disaster Management Office of the Kagoshima prefectural government said. The typhoon is expected to strike the Japanese mainland on Sunday. The latest typhoon to hit the region in recent weeks, Jelawat is a "very strong" storm with maximum sustained winds near the center of just over 100 miles per hour, the Japan Meteorological Agency said. A NASA advisory said the cyclone was comparable to a category 3 hurricane. The cyclone has lost some of its might and should continue weakening after moving into colder waters, said CNN meteorologist Karen Maginnis. Wind troughs out of China could divert Jelawat away from land and into the open Pacific Ocean.

71. (   ) What is the speaker mainly discussing?
    (A) Entertainment.
    (B) Geography.
    (C) Economics.
    (D) Weather.

72. (   ) What happened in Okinawa?
    (A) It was struck by a tornado.
    (B) At least 50 people were injured.
    (C) Only three people were injured.
    (D) Five people were killed.

73. (   ) What did NOT happen in Japan?
    (A) Many homes lost electricity.
    (B) There were strong winds.
    (C) People were injured.
    (D) The government declared an emergency.

GO ON TO THE NEXT PAGE.

Good afternoon. As you know, my name is Nan Peck, and I'm pleased to talk with you about a topic that is near and dear to my head and my heart: listening skills. Your president tells me that this is important to you as well. Let me ask you this: On a scale of 1 to 10, how would you rate yourself as a listener? Most U.S. adults would rate themselves a 7.5. Unfortunately, according to the National Communication Association, if you're like most adults, you listen with just 25% efficiency! If you're like me, you realize that there is more to listening than meets the ear. If you're like me, you know that it's in your best interests to improve your listening skills. I've been studying listening and training people to improve their listening skills for more than 20 years. I spent 14 years training listeners for a suicide hotline and other professionals who recognize the importance of good listening. For the next thirty minutes, I'd like to share with you the five important listening considerations that I believe will help you get along better with your family and friends, and your colleagues. With the hope that you'll be actively listening to me, I invite you to stop me at any time and to ask me for clarification. I promise to listen to you, too.

74. (   ) Who is the speaker?
    (A) An expert on statistics.
    (B) An expert on communication.
    (C) An expert on corporate management.
    (D) An expert on body language.

75. (   ) What will the speaker talk about?
    (A) Listening skills.
    (B) Speaking skills.
    (C) Study habits.
    (D) Management styles.

76. (   ) When can the audience ask questions?
    (A) At the end of the speech.
    (B) Before the speech begins.
    (C) 30 minutes later.
    (D) Any time.

OK, Bulls fans! Can I have your attention, please? We're about to announce the winner of tonight's Lucky Winner drawing. If your seat number is called, you'll win a fantastic prize package consisting of a Chicago Bulls team jacket, an autographed Derrick Rose poster, a $50 gift certificate to Big Al's Restaurant, and two tickets to an upcoming Bulls' game. OK, get your tickets out. Tonight's lucky winner is sitting in... section 2, row 12, and seat... 23! Do we have a winner? Yes! There he is on the big screen. OK, great! So listen, buddy, to claim your prize, bring your ticket to the fan information booth adjacent to tunnel 28 before the end of the game. The rest of you, remember to keep your ticket stub from tonight's game. It entitles you to $5 off a regular wash and wax at any Pink Panda Car Wash location.

77. (   ) Where is this announcement being made?
    (A) At a sports stadium.
    (B) In an airport.
    (C) In a restaurant.
    (D) At a public auction.

78. (   ) What is the speaker offering?
    (A) A prize package.
    (B) An internship.
    (C) An autographed basketball.
    (D) A chance to play for the Bulls.

79. (   ) Which of the following is NOT mentioned by the speaker?
    (A) Big Al's Restaurant.
    (B) Derrick Rose.
    (C) Pink Panda Car Wash.
    (D) The name of the winner.

GO ON TO THE NEXT PAGE.

This is Anna Stasha with your KKP-FM traffic and weather on the ones. It's still early, folks, but so far so good out on the roads this morning, with no major delays to report. You're looking at standard commute times all over the tri-county area. However, starting tomorrow, the department of transportation will close the two left lanes of I-45 between Fuller Road and the Franken Freeway, in both directions. No word on what's going on there. Just avoid it if possible. Today's weather is as pleasant and predictable as today's traffic report, with clear skies and temps in the upper 70s, with maybe a slight breeze off the lake. Tonight, clear skies, lows in the mid-to-upper 60s. Tomorrow and the rest of the week look good, with no major storm fronts headed our way. Visit KKP's website for up-to-date traffic and weather conditions. This segment of KKP's traffic and weather was brought to you by State Farm Insurance. Like a good neighbor, State Farm is there. I'm Anna Stasha and now back to Rick and Dick's Morning Zoo.

80. (   ) When was this report made?
      (A) In the early morning.
      (B) In the afternoon.
      (C) At noon.
      (D) In the evening.

81. (   ) What will happen tomorrow?
      (A) It will rain.
      (B) Lane closures on I-45.
      (C) A slight breeze off the lake.
      (D) A parade on Fuller Road.

82. (   ) Where would this report be heard?
      (A) On the radio.
      (B) In a newspaper.
      (C) On the Internet.
      (D) On the voice mail system.

Hi, Claire, it's David. Listen, I know you said you want to go to the Honest Traders store in Polk City tomorrow, but we'd have to get up awfully early to do that. You know I need to be back by one, right? I think it would be better to leave around nine or ten. There's another Honest Traders in Freeport. I know it's a longer trip, but we'd still have plenty of time to shop. It also seems like the buses run more regularly throughout the day, so we'd have no trouble getting back. Give me a call back and let me know what you think.

83. (   ) What does David suggest?
     (A) Leaving early for Honest Traders.
     (B) Going to Honest Traders after one o'clock.
     (C) Leaving for Polk City later in the day.
     (D) Going to a different place than planned.

84. (   ) What is the disadvantage of going to Freeport?
     (A) It is farther away.
     (B) It is difficult to return from.
     (C) It is too crowded.
     (D) The store has limited hours.

85. (   ) Look at the graphic. Which bus would David like to take?
     (A) The 10:15 to Trallee.
     (B) The 7:00 to Polk City.
     (C) The 12:00 to Milltown.
     (D) The 9:30 to Freeport.

County Bus Routes			
Avery	8:00	9:15	4:30	5:15
Casper	7:00	7:15	7:30	8:00
Freeport	8:00	9:30	11:00	12:30
Milltown	8:00	10:00	12:00	2:00
Polk City	6:30	7:00	12:00	3:00
Trallee	8:15	9:15	10:15	11:15

GO ON TO THE NEXT PAGE.

Ladies and gentlemen, the Captain has turned on the Fasten Seat Belt sign. If you haven't already done so, please stow your carry-on luggage underneath the seat in front of you or in an overhead bin. Please take your seat and fasten your seat belt. And also make sure your seat back and folding tray are in their full upright position. If you are seated next to an emergency exit, please read the special instructions card located by your seat carefully. If, in the event of an emergency, you do not wish to perform the functions described, please ask a flight attendant to reseat you. At this time, we request that all mobile phones, pagers, radios and remote controlled toys be turned off for the full duration of the flight, as these items might interfere with the navigational and communication equipment on this aircraft. We request that all other electronic devices be turned off until we fly above 10,000 feet. We will notify you when it is safe to use such devices. We remind you that this is a non-smoking flight. Smoking is prohibited on the entire aircraft, including the lavatories. Tampering with, disabling or destroying the lavatory smoke detectors is prohibited by law. If you have any questions about our flight today, please don't hesitate to ask one of our flight attendants. Thank you.

86. (   ) What is prohibited by law?
    (A) Using laptops in the cabin.
    (B) Tampering with smoke detectors.
    (C) Listening to music on the flight.
    (D) Carry-on luggage.

87. (   ) Where does this announcement take place?
    (A) On an airplane.
    (B) At a business meeting.
    (C) On television.
    (D) In a bus station.

88. (   ) What should listeners do if they have a question?
    (A) Call the airline.
    (B) Ask a flight attendant.
    (C) Go to the lavatory.
    (D) Complain to the manager.

Before we begin the lecture, I'd like to tell you a little bit about myself. I was born in Russia and moved to the United States with my family when I was three. My father was a doctor, and my mother was a teacher. I have two older brothers and a younger sister. I grew up in Boston, but we moved to Chicago when I was 12. I've been interested in science my whole life, so I was ecstatic to receive a scholarship here at Northwestern University to study biology. After earning my bachelor's degree, I got a master's at Stanford. I stayed on there as a researcher for about six years before moving back to Illinois and joining Bio-Tech. I was with Bio-Tech for 10 years before leaving last year to start my own research company, GreenEarth. We employ six full-time researchers, and in the past year we've made a couple of exciting new discoveries, which I'm going to tell you about in just a minute. First, though, I just want to thank the Northwestern president, John Roche, and the faculty of the biology department for inviting me back to speak to you today. It's an exciting moment, and I'm honored.

89. (   ) What will the speaker most likely talk about next?
    (A) Sports.
    (B) The weather.
    (C) Biology.
    (D) Economics.

90. (   ) Where did the speaker obtain his master's degree?
    (A) Bio-Tech.
    (B) University of Illinois.
    (C) Northwestern University.
    (D) Stanford University.

91. (   ) Where was the speaker born?
    (A) Boston.
    (B) Chicago.
    (C) Russia.
    (D) Illinois.

GO ON TO THE NEXT PAGE.

Have you heard the story about the donkey who is trying to choose between two bales of hay? Both bales of hay are equal in all respects. Size, quality, amount, fragrance, you name it. Absolutely no difference between the two. So the donkey, he's standing there and he looks left. There's a perfectly good bale of hay. Then he looks right. Aha! Another beautiful bale of hay. This poor donkey, he's so confused that he doesn't know what to do—so he doesn't do anything. He stands there between the two bales of hay and starves to death. Think of the average consumer as being that proverbial donkey. The average consumer is so overwhelmed by choice that he can't make a decision. And it's your job, it's your mission, it's your passion, to create a bale of hay so incredibly superior to the others that no donkey in his right mind would pass it up. And if it isn't your passion, then you should walk out of this seminar, demand a refund at the registration desk, and go back to being that indecisive little donkey, because I'm wasting your time here.

92. (   ) Who is the speaker?
   (A) A preacher.
   (B) An animal therapist.
   (C) An author of comic books.
   (D) An advertising professional.

93. (   ) Why does the speaker tell the story of the donkey?
   (A) To draw a comparison.
   (B) To explain a procedure.
   (C) To clarify a statement.
   (D) To insult an audience member.

94. (   ) What does the speaker say about average consumers?
   (A) They look like donkeys.
   (B) They are overwhelmed by choice.
   (C) They prefer smaller bales of hay.
   (D) They have a passion for creativity.

Well, to be honest, George, my main inspiration came from being so disappointed with customer service from other computer companies. For years I had a Bell PC and anytime something went wrong, resolving the issue was a nightmare. Their tech support and customer service was pathetic. And so I thought, well, you know, if you want something done right, you have to do it yourself. I know it's clichéd but I really believed that I could do a better job than the guys who are now my direct competitors. Consumers want companies and brands that they believe will deliver on their promises. That's where I felt like I could make a difference: in customer service, because if we can provide a higher level of customer service, that inspires trust in our consumers, and gives us a competitive advantage.

95. (   ) What is the speaker mainly discussing?
　　　(A) His reason for starting a business.
　　　(B) His political views.
　　　(C) His experience with computers.
　　　(D) His opinion of the computer industry.

96. (   ) What does the speaker say about consumers?
　　　(A) They don't care about customer service.
　　　(B) They prefer reliable companies.
　　　(C) They give him a competitive edge.
　　　(D) They always think they can do a better job.

97. (   ) What does the speaker imply about his company?
　　　(A) They provide a high level of customer service.
　　　(B) They are most concerned with competitive pricing.
　　　(C) They are struggling.
　　　(D) They are wildly profitable.

GO ON TO THE NEXT PAGE.

As all Americans know, the Fourth of July isn't really about being patriotic—it's an excuse to have a rooftop or backyard barbeque, to consume copious amounts of alcohol, and to watch some fantastic fireworks. So what are Americans living in Taipei supposed to do in place of these time-honored traditions? For starters, don't expect fireworks. But DO look forward to having drinks with friends at Dazzling Champagne bar's 4th of July party. Free shots will be served to anyone wearing red, white, and blue. So grab your friends, and if they're not American, brief them on why July 4th is a special day and come join us at Dazzling Champagne for a night of fun and celebration! Admission is free and appetizers will be served.

98. (   ) What is the purpose of this announcement?
    (A) To announce an event.
    (B) To sell a product.
    (C) To start an argument.
    (D) To introduce a speaker.

99. (   ) What is implied about the 4th of July?
    (A) It's a minor religious holiday.
    (B) It's an important American holiday.
    (C) It's an excuse to set fires.
    (D) It's a reason to become an American.

100. (   ) What should customers do if they want a free shot?
    (A) Bring at least three friends.
    (B) Buy an appetizer.
    (C) Wear something red, white, and blue.
    (D) Pay the admission fee in advance.

TOEIC ANSWER SHEET

REGISTRATION No.

姓 名
N A M E

LISTENING SECTION

Part 1

No.	ANSWER A B C D
1	A B C D
2	A B C D
3	A B C D
4	A B C D
5	A B C D
6	A B C D
7	A B C
8	A B C
9	A B C
10	A B C

Part 2

No.	ANSWER A B C D
11	A B C
12	A B C
13	A B C
14	A B C
15	A B C
16	A B C
17	A B C
18	A B C
19	A B C
20	A B C

No.	ANSWER A B C D
21	A B C
22	A B C
23	A B C
24	A B C
25	A B C
26	A B C
27	A B C
28	A B C
29	A B C
30	A B C

Part 3

No.	ANSWER A B C D
31	A B C
32	A B C D
33	A B C D
34	A B C D
35	A B C D
36	A B C D
37	A B C D
38	A B C D
39	A B C D
40	A B C D

No.	ANSWER A B C D
41	A B C D
42	A B C D
43	A B C D
44	A B C D
45	A B C D
46	A B C D
47	A B C D
48	A B C D
49	A B C D
50	A B C D

No.	ANSWER A B C D
51	A B C D
52	A B C D
53	A B C D
54	A B C D
55	A B C D
56	A B C D
57	A B C D
58	A B C D
59	A B C D
60	A B C D

Part 4

No.	ANSWER A B C D
61	A B C D
62	A B C D
63	A B C D
64	A B C D
65	A B C D
66	A B C D
67	A B C D
68	A B C D
69	A B C D
70	A B C D

No.	ANSWER A B C D
71	A B C D
72	A B C D
73	A B C D
74	A B C D
75	A B C D
76	A B C D
77	A B C D
78	A B C D
79	A B C D
80	A B C D

No.	ANSWER A B C D
81	A B C D
82	A B C D
83	A B C D
84	A B C D
85	A B C D
86	A B C D
87	A B C D
88	A B C D
89	A B C D
90	A B C D

No.	ANSWER A B C D
91	A B C D
92	A B C D
93	A B C D
94	A B C D
95	A B C D
96	A B C D
97	A B C D
98	A B C D
99	A B C D
100	A B C D

READING SECTION

Part 5

No.	ANSWER A B C D
101	A B C D
102	A B C D
103	A B C D
104	A B C D
105	A B C D
106	A B C D
107	A B C D
108	A B C D
109	A B C D
110	A B C D

No.	ANSWER A B C D
111	A B C D
112	A B C D
113	A B C D
114	A B C D
115	A B C D
116	A B C D
117	A B C D
118	A B C D
119	A B C D
120	A B C D

No.	ANSWER A B C D
121	A B C D
122	A B C D
123	A B C D
124	A B C D
125	A B C D
126	A B C D
127	A B C D
128	A B C D
129	A B C D
130	A B C D

Part 6

No.	ANSWER A B C D
131	A B C D
132	A B C D
133	A B C D
134	A B C D
135	A B C D
136	A B C D
137	A B C D
138	A B C D
139	A B C D
140	A B C D

No.	ANSWER A B C D
141	A B C D
142	A B C D
143	A B C D
144	A B C D
145	A B C D
146	A B C D
147	A B C D
148	A B C D
149	A B C D
150	A B C D

Part 7

No.	ANSWER A B C D
151	A B C D
152	A B C D
153	A B C D
154	A B C D
155	A B C D
156	A B C D
157	A B C D
158	A B C D
159	A B C D
160	A B C D

No.	ANSWER A B C D
161	A B C D
162	A B C D
163	A B C D
164	A B C D
165	A B C D
166	A B C D
167	A B C D
168	A B C D
169	A B C D
170	A B C D

No.	ANSWER A B C D
171	A B C D
172	A B C D
173	A B C D
174	A B C D
175	A B C D
176	A B C D
177	A B C D
178	A B C D
179	A B C D
180	A B C D

No.	ANSWER A B C D
181	A B C D
182	A B C D
183	A B C D
184	A B C D
185	A B C D
186	A B C D
187	A B C D
188	A B C D
189	A B C D
190	A B C D

No.	ANSWER A B C D
191	A B C D
192	A B C D
193	A B C D
194	A B C D
195	A B C D
196	A B C D
197	A B C D
198	A B C D
199	A B C D
200	A B C D

「多益獎學金」申請辦法：

★凡向學習出版公司團訂New TOEIC Model Test課堂教材的同學，參加TOEIC測驗，成績達下列標準，可申請以下獎學金。

分　數	獎　學　金
990分滿分	2萬元現金支票
950分以上	1萬元現金支票
900分以上	5,000元現金支票
800分以上	1,000元現金支票
700分以上	500元現金支票

1. 同一級分獎學金，不得重複申請；申請第二次獎學金時，則須先扣除已領取的部份，補足差額。
   例如：某生第一次參加多益測驗，得分825，可申請獎學金1,000元，之後第二次參加測驗，得分950，則某生可領取
   10,000元－1,000元＝9,000元獎學金差額。

2. 若同學申請第一次獎學金後，考第二次成績比第一次差，雖仍達到申請獎學金標準，將不得再申請獎學金。

3. 申請同學須於上課期間，憑成績單申請，並有授課老師簽名。

【本活動於2021年12月31日截止】